W9-CJT-523

Lothrop, Lee & Shepard Books   New York

Copyright © 1988 by John Steptoe.
All rights reserved. No part of this book may be reproduced or utilized in
any form or by any means, electronic or mechanical, including
photocopying, recording or by any information storage and retrieval
system, without permission in writing from the Publisher. Inquiries should
be addressed to Lothrop, Lee & Shepard Books, a division of William
Morrow & Company, Inc., 1350 Avenue of the Americas, New York,
New York 10019.
Printed in Singapore.
7 8 9 10

Library of Congress Cataloging in Publication Data
Steptoe, John, 1950-   Baby says.
Summary: A baby and big brother figure out how to get along.
[1. Brothers—Fiction. 2. Babies—Fiction.
3. Afro-Americans—Fiction] I. Title. PZ7.S8367Bab
1988   [E]   87-17296   ISBN 0-688-07423-5   ISBN 0-688-07424-3 (lib. bdg.)

Baby Says

John Steptoe

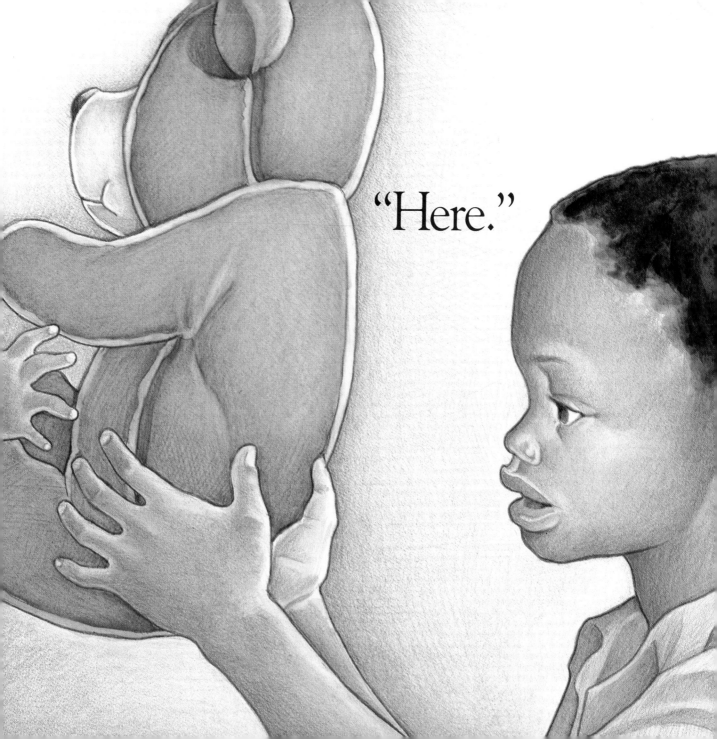

"Here."

"Uh, oh."

"No, no."

"No, no!"

"Okay, okay."

"Okay.
Uh, oh.
No, no."

"Uh, oh.
No, no."

"Okay, baby.
Okay."

Baby says,
"Okay!"